P9-DHH-310

Oh, Bother! SOMEONE'S AFRAID OF THE DARK!

By Betty Birney
Illustrated by Darrell Baker

A GOLDEN BOOK • NEW YORK
Western Publishing Company, Inc., Racine, Wisconsin 53404

 Library of Congress Catalog Card Number: 93-78958 ISBN: 0-307-12843-1/ISBN: 0-307-62843-4 (lib. bdg.) MCMXCIV

The sun was setting as Winnie the Pooh and Piglet headed home after a day of exploring in the Hundred-Acre Wood.

"Piglet, it was a wonderful day," said Pooh. "Of course, every day is wonderful if you have a full jar of honey."

Pooh peered into the jar he was carrying.

"Oh, bother!" he said. "My full jar of honey is almost empty."

"Look," Piglet said. "Tigger and Owl are pitching a tent under the trees."

"Hi, Pooh and Piglet!" Tigger shouted to them. "I've talked Owl into camping out tonight!"

"That sounds like fun, doesn't it, Piglet?" said Pooh as he stopped to wave to their friends.

"No, it doesn't," Piglet answered quickly, and he went right on walking.

Pooh caught up with Piglet. Soon they reached a fork in the path. It was time to say good night, but Piglet did not want Pooh to leave.

"Walk home with me," Piglet begged Pooh. "You can sleep over. We'll camp *inside* tonight. Please?"

Pooh had never heard of camping inside before.

"I have a full jar of honey at home," offered Piglet.

"Sounds like a good idea," said Pooh, patting his tummy. "Let's go!"

As they arrived at Piglet's house, Pooh stopped and pointed up to the sky.

"Look, Piglet. There's the first star!" said Pooh.

"Let's get inside—quick!" said Piglet, whose only thought was that the night was getting dark very fast.

"But I have to make a wish," Pooh protested as Piglet pulled him in the door.

When they were inside the house, Pooh was surprised to see Piglet push a large table in front of the door. "What are you doing?" he asked.

"Can't be too careful," Piglet answered.

"Oh?" said Pooh. He wasn't sure what Piglet meant, but he didn't ask any more questions. He was too busy wondering about Piglet's jar of honey.

Pooh and Piglet settled down for a pleasant evening at home. First Piglet worked on a jigsaw puzzle and Pooh ate honey.

The puzzle reminded Piglet of something. So he told the story about three little piglets and Pooh ate honey.

Then Pooh told about the huge honeybee that he had followed the previous spring. "I knew there would be gallons of honey waiting just for me because the bee was *this* big," said Pooh, holding up his paws. "Then, sadly, the bee just disappeared."

After Piglet told Pooh how much he enjoyed the honeybee story, the two friends sang songs.

Before Pooh knew it, the honey was all gone and he was feeling very tired. "I think I'd like to go to sleep now, Piglet," he said.

However, Piglet still didn't want to go to bed. He suggested that they finish the evening with a game of haycorn checkers.

Pooh tried to play, but he just couldn't stay awake any longer. "All right, Pooh," Piglet said with a sigh. "I guess it *is* time to go to bed."

Before they went to bed, Pooh and Piglet brushed their teeth.

Standing at the washbasin, Piglet suddenly saw a horrible sight. It was the shadow of a huge creature with a gigantic stick in his hand!

"P-p-pooh," whispered Piglet, trembling. "There's a heffible Horralump . . . I mean a Lumpaheff . . . Oh, dear. Well, something awful is about to get us!"

Pooh looked around and saw the shadow on the wall. He waved his toothbrush at it.

"Look, it's waving back at me," said Pooh. "Why, it *is* me. Actually it's my shadow."

"Oh," said Piglet. "I guess you're right."

At last Pooh and Piglet were ready to go to sleep. "I think I'll just check under the bed for Heffalumps," said Piglet.

"Do you see any?" Pooh asked.

"No," Piglet admitted. "But that doesn't mean they're not there."

Piglet climbed into bed at last. Pooh yawned and switched off the lamp.

"You can't turn off the lamp!" said Piglet, turning it back on again. "We need it on—to keep the Heffalumps away."

"But, Piglet—you blocked the door. A Heffalump can't get in," Pooh reminded his friend, and he gave Piglet a reassuring pat.

"I hope you're right," said Piglet uncertainly as he switched off the lamp.

Pooh fell asleep immediately, but Piglet stayed wide awake.

"Pooh," he whispered, "I hear something."

Pooh did not answer.

"Pooh!" whispered Piglet a little louder this time. "It's definitely a Heffalump-something."

Pooh still did not answer, so Piglet gave Pooh a push and said, "There's a Heffalump right in this room! Don't you hear him going *tick tock, tick tock*?"

"Huh?" said Pooh, awake at last. "Oh, yes, I do. Don't worry, Piglet. I'll get him!"

Pooh grabbed his pillow, stood up, and pounced on the Heffalump. "Got you!" he shouted.

Then Pooh switched on the lamp and lifted up the pillow. "What do you know!" Pooh said. "A Heffalump looks just like an alarm clock!"

"Oh, it *is* an alarm clock," said Piglet, very relieved.

Pooh thought for a moment. "Piglet," he said. "If I didn't know better, I'd think you are afraid of the dark!"

"Well, there are scary things in the dark," Piglet replied. "Like Heffalumps and Jagulars."

"But, Piglet, we haven't actually seen a Heffalump, have we?" said Pooh.

"We thought we saw one, but it was really your shadow," Piglet admitted. "Then we thought we heard one, but it was really the clock."

Piglet continued, “I guess Heffalumps are just in my imagination.”

“I guess that’s true,” said Pooh. “So there’s nothing to be afraid of anymore.”

Suddenly there was a knock at the door. Piglet didn’t want to answer it, but Pooh said he would go and ask who was there. Piglet decided it would be safer if he followed Pooh.

"Who is it?" asked Pooh at the front door.

From outside a voice answered, "It's Tigger and Owl, Pooh."

Suddenly Piglet hid under the table and began shaking with fear. "Tigger and a Howling Boo!" he whispered. "That's worse than a Heffalump!"

Pooh was puzzled. "That didn't sound like a Howling Boo," he said out loud. "It sounded like someone we know. Think, think, think."

"You're right," said Piglet. "I've heard that voice before."

"It sounded like Owl," said Pooh. "He was saying, 'It's Tigger and Owl, Pooh.'"

"If it's only Tigger and Owl, there's nothing to be afraid of," said Piglet, greatly relieved once more.

Pooh helped Piglet push the table away. When they opened the door, Owl and Tigger were standing outside in the light of a firefly lantern.

"Come on out!" said Tigger, bouncing excitedly. "There's something you've got to see."

"Isn't it awfully *dark* out there?" asked Piglet, who was still a little bit nervous.

"But wait until you see the lights in the sky," said Owl.

When Piglet and Pooh stepped outside, they saw that the sky was filled with glittering stars.

"Those star pictures in the sky are constellations," said Owl, looking up at the sky. "There's the Big Bear. And over there is the Little Bear."

"Oh, yes," said Pooh, "and I think I see a Big Honey Jar and a Little Honey Jar!"

"Show him that Tiggerific picture," said Tigger, bouncing impatiently.

"Piglet," said Owl, pointing a wing upward. "We think that constellation right up there looks like you."

"Why, it *does* look like me!" cried Piglet, staring at the night sky and forgetting all about being afraid.

The four friends watched the starry sky for a long time.

Pooh put his arm around Piglet. "No need to be afraid of the dark anymore," he said. "Now that you know you have a friendly piglet looking down on you."

"You're right," said Piglet. "And that piglet doesn't look scared of the dark at all!"